139923

A Beginning-to-Read Book

Dear Dragon Goes Camping

by Margaret Hillert
Illustrated by David Schimmell

NORWOOD HOUSE PRESS

DEAR CAREGIVER,

The *Beginning-to-Read* series is a carefully written collection of classic readers you may remember from your own childhood. Each book features text comprised of common sight words to provide your child ample practice reading the words that appear most frequently in written text. The many additional details in the pictures enhance the story and offer the opportunity for you to help your child expand oral language and develop comprehension.

Begin by reading the story to your child, followed by letting him or her read familiar words and soon your child will be able to read the story independently. At each step of the way, be sure to praise your reader's efforts to build his or her confidence as an independent reader. Discuss the pictures and encourage your child to make connections between the story and his or her own life. At the end of the story, you will find reading activities and a word list that will help your child practice and strengthen beginning reading skills.

Above all, the most important part of the reading experience is to have fun and enjoy it!

Shannon Cannon

Shannon Cannon,
Literacy Consultant

Norwood House Press • P.O. Box 316598 • Chicago, Illinois 60631
For more information about Norwood House Press please visit our website at
www.norwoodhousepress.com or call 866-565-2900.

Text copyright ©2011 by Margaret Hillert. Illustrations and cover design copyright ©2011 by Norwood House Press, Inc. All rights reserved. No part of this book may be reproduced or utilized in any form or by any means without written permission from the publisher.

LIBRARY OF CONGRESS CATALOGING-IN-PUBLICATION DATA

Hillert, Margaret.
    Dear dragon goes camping / by Margaret Hillert ; illustrated by David Schimmell.
        p. cm. -- (A beginning-to-read book)
    Summary: "A boy and his pet dragon go exploring and have fun on a family camping trip"--Provided by publisher.
    ISBN-13: 978-1-59953-345-2 (library edition : alk. paper)
    ISBN-10: 1-59953-345-6 (library edition : alk. paper)
    [1. Camping--Fiction. 2. Dragons--Fiction.] I. Schimmell, David, ill. II. Title.
    PZ7.H558De 2010
    [E]--dc22
                            2009034532

Manufactured in the United States of America in North Mankato, Minnesota.
182R—042011

Come here.
Come here.
You can help me do this.

Where will we go, Mother?
Where will we go?

Away, away to a good spot.
You will like it.
Get in the car.

Oh, boy.
This is fun.
Away, away we go.

JC 8074

Campin

And here we are.
This is the spot.

I can help, Father.
I am pretty big now.
I can help do this.

We will put up this big one for
you and Mother.
We will put up this little one for me.

I want to go for a walk, Father.
Maybe I can find something for Mother.

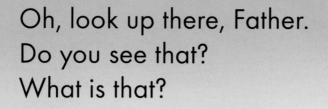

Oh, look up there, Father.
Do you see that?
What is that?

That owl?
Is that what you see?
The owl likes it up there.
It wants us to go away.

Oh, here is something.
What a pretty leaf.
Mother will like it.

Mother. Mother.
Look at this pretty red
and yellow leaf.
I want you to have it.

And I want you to have
something good to eat.

Oh, you can help with this.
You are good at it.
Come on.
Do it. Do it.
Make a fire.

Oh, boy.
You are so good at this.
Now we can make something to eat.

Look at this.
This is what I like.

Ummm— this is so good, good, good.

This is good, too.
I will eat one.
Maybe two—
maybe three!

See the moon come up.
The moon is so big and yellow.
So pretty.

Now we will go in here.
It will be fun.

Here I am with you.
And here you are with me.
Oh, what a good, good day, dear dragon.

The following activities support the findings of the National Reading Panel that determined the most effective components for reading instruction are: Phonemic Awareness, Phonics, Vocabulary, Fluency, and Text Comprehension.

Phonemic Awareness: The suffix -ing

Oral Blending:

1. Say the suffix *-ing* and ask your child to repeat it.

2. Say the following words and ask your child to add the *-ing* suffix to the end to make a new word:

jump + ing = jumping	pack + ing = packing	lift + ing = lifting
do + ing = doing	work + ing = working	eat + ing = eating
cook + ing = cooking	walk + ing = walking	sleep + ing = sleeping
help + ing = helping	pick + ing = picking	play + ing = playing

Phonics: The suffix -ing

1. Explain to your child that a suffix is a group of letters that is added to the end of a base word. For example, when *-ing* is added to the word **camp**, it becomes **camping**.

2. Write the following words on separate pieces of paper: jumping, packing, lifting, doing, working, eating, cooking, walking, sleeping, helping, picking, playing.

3. Read each word and ask your child to underline the base word.

4. Cut the words in half, separating the *-ing* suffix from the base word. Turn the pieces of paper face down to play a game in which you take turns picking two pieces of paper to see if you can match a base word with a suffix. If you pick two base words or two suffixes, turn them back over. Continue playing until you have matched all of the words and suffixes.

Vocabulary: Concept Words

1. Fold a piece of paper in half the long way.

2. Draw a line down the fold to divide the paper in two parts.

3. Write the words **At Home** and **At Camp** in separate columns at the top of the page.

4. Write the following nouns on separate pieces of paper:

sleeping bag	tent	yard	stove	log
house	fire	woods	bed	chair

5. Read the words aloud and ask your child whether each one belongs in the **At Home** or **At Camp** column. Write the words in each column or ask your child to write the words in each column.

6. Mix up the words and ask your child to match one **At Home** word with one **At Camp** word (bed/sleeping bag, tent/house, woods/yard, fire/stove, log/chair).

Fluency: Echo Reading

1. Reread the story to your child at least two more times as your child tracks the print by running a finger under the words as they are read. Ask your child to read the words he or she knows with you.

2. Reread the story, stopping after each sentence or page to allow your child to read (echo) what you have read. Repeat echo reading and let your child take the lead.

Text Comprehension: Discussion Time

1. Ask your child to retell the sequence of events in the story.

2. To check comprehension, ask your child the following questions:

- How did the boy help his mother and father?
- What did the boy find for his mother?
- How did they cook food in the story?
- Would you like to go camping? Why?

WORD LIST

Dear Dragon Goes Camping uses the 72 words listed below.
This list can be used to practice reading the words that appear in the text.
You may wish to write the words on index cards and use them to help your
child build automatic word recognition. Regular practice with these words
will enhance your child's fluency in reading connected text.

a	eat	it	pretty	up
am			put	us
and	Father	leaf		
are	find	like(s)	red	walk
at	fire	little		want(s)
away	for	look		we
	fun		see	what
be		make	so	where
big	get	maybe	something	will
boy	go	me	spot	with
	good	moon	that	
can		Mother	the	yellow
car	have		there	you
come	help	now	this	
	here		three	
day		oh	to	
dear	I	on	too	
do	in	one	two	
dragon	is	owl		

ABOUT THE AUTHOR Margaret Hillert has written over 80 books for
children who are just learning to read. Her books
have been translated into many different languages and over a million children
throughout the world have read her books. She first started writing poetry as
a child and has continued to write for children and adults throughout her life. A
first grade teacher for 34 years, Margaret is now retired from teaching and lives in
Michigan where she likes to write, take walks in the morning, and care for her three cats.

Photograph by Glenna Washburn

ABOUT THE ADVISER Shannon Cannon contributed the activities pages that appear in
this book. Shannon serves as a literacy consultant and provides
staff development to help improve reading instruction. She is a frequent presenter at educational
conferences and workshops. Prior to this she worked as an elementary school teacher and as
president of a curriculum publishing company.